STAR✳BEASTS

STAR✶BEASTS

WRITTEN BY
STEPHANIE YOUNG

ILLUSTRATED BY
ALLYSON LASSITER

ONI PRESS

AN ONI PRESS PUBLICATION

CAPTAIN BANDIT

Good dog at heart
and the Star Beasts'
youngest Captain

COMMANDER FLASHTISTA

Kick-asteroid warrior
turtle and the *Condor*'s
BLAST YEAH pilot

SIR IAN MACCABRAN

Nickname: Macca
Zoorb Councilor, Unicorn
Knight, and last of his kind

CREWCREATURE DR. MARIA CURLY

Ambitious sheep,
respected scientist,
and math wiz

LIEUTENANT KARMA JAMYANG

Caring healer, common-sense
medic, and peaceful tiger

ZAYD OF THE SERENGETI

Go-with-the-flow Zebra, galactic DJ, and Star Beasts Ambassador

LIEUTENANT CLIO FIN

Librarian goldfish, dedicated scholar, and swimming in historical facts

CREWCREATURE ELEANOR LA

Creative parakeet, artistic innovator, and problem-solver

CREWCREATURE SNUFFS LEWIS

Practical pig, space farmer, and grows far-out veggies

RECRUIT PEPITO

Nickname: Pep
Techie iguana, happy helper, and gadget geek

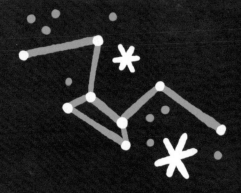

Written by STEPHANIE YOUNG

Illustrated by ALLYSON LASSITER

Colors by LISA HADLEY & ALLYSON LASSITER

Lassie Font Created by LILA SYMONS
at ALPHABETS AT WORK

Designed by SONJA SYNAK

Edited by AMANDA MEADOWS

PUBLISHED BY ONI-LION FORGE PUBLISHING GROUP, LLC

James Lucas Jones, president & publisher
Sarah Gaydos, editor in chief • Charlie Chu,
e.v.p. of creative & business development
Brad Rooks, director of operations • Amber
O'Neill, special projects manager • Margot Wood,
director of marketing & sales • Katie Sainz,
marketing manager • Tara Lehmann, publicist
Holly Aitchison, consumer marketing manager
Troy Look, director of design & production • Kate Z.
Stone, senior graphic designer • Hilary Thompson,
graphic designer • Carey Hall, graphic designer
Sarah Rockwell, graphic designer • Angie
Knowles, digital prepress lead • Vincent Kukua,
digital prepress technician • Jasmine Amiri,
senior editor • Shawna Gore, senior editor
Amanda Meadows, senior editor • Robert Meyers,
senior editor, licensing • Desiree Rodriguez, editor
Grace Scheipeter, editor • Zack Soto, editor
Chris Cerasi, editorial coordinator • Steve
Ellis, vice president of games • Ben Eisner,
game developer • Michelle Nguyen, executive
assistant • Jung Lee, logistics coordinator

Joe Nozemack, publisher emeritus

1319 SE Martin Luther King Jr. Blvd.
Suite 240
Portland, OR 97214

ONIPRESS.COM
 @onipress
 @onipress
 @onipress
 @onipress

STARBEASTSCOMIC.WORDPRESS.COM
 @allysonlassiter @sfarrisyoung

First Edition: August 2021
ISBN 978-1-62010-937-3
eISBN 978-1-62010-950-2

1 2 3 4 5 6 7 8 9 10

Library of Congress Control Number
2021934310

Printed in Canada.

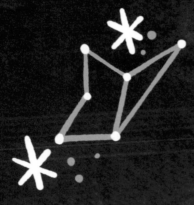

For Pickles
and Mr. Whiskers

Only the bravest creatures are chosen to be Star Beasts, the protectors of Earth...

And they chose me?

One day I'll come back. I promise.

CHAPTER 1

Lagoonta, Capital Planet of the Crocodile Empire

Don't worry, Star Beasts. This security check-in will be a piece of pupcake.

Uh, Karma? Should I be worried?

zzzzz-SNORT-zzzzz

No, Pep. The Crocs are cool. Captain Bandit's never been to Lagoonta before.

Lagoonta Crocs are Earth's oldest allies. I'll just introduce myself, then—

FINALLY. No more rehearsing! Say "Hi" to them and get it over with.

Practicing is a good idea, Captain. Lagoontans are proud perfectionists.

I'm not bowing to no snooty Crocs. Pep and I'll hang back with the ship.

If that's how you feel, Flashtista, I guess that's okay.

Away crew, let's say hello to some Crocodiles.

FLASHTISTA! PICK US UP!

Buckle up, Pep!

Stellarspeed us outta this swamp!

Sorry, crew. I don't know what went wrong back there.

It's crystal clear!

A GOOD captain would prepare for anything! A GOOD captain would protect his crew!

Protect the crew?!?

Maria, I've ordered you to finish the *Condor*'s new cloaking system EIGHT times now!

DON'T CALL ME MARIA. IT'S DOCTOR. DR. MARIA CURLY!

Captain, history couldn't have predicted that attack.

Yeah, Clio's right! Earth and Lagoonta are BFFs. It's a for real fact!

FACT? Here's a fact!

You have less Star Beasts experience than anyone on the *Condor* EXCEPT the kid iguana!

I've been a Star Beasts scientist since I was a lamb!

Trust me. It's not *logical* to call you "CAPTAIN" of ANYTHING!

Then don't call me "Captain." I like "Bandit" better, anyway.

CLICK. CLICKTY-CLICK. CLICK. CLICK...

CLICK. CLICK. CLICKTY...

Bandit?

Stupid space junk!

Uh... Captain?

Go ahead, Pep.

um. I'm beaming in a video call from the, UH, Star Beasts Zoorb Council.

Councilor Thunderbird. What's the news from Earth?

It's the news from Lagoonta that concerns me.

That just happened! How did the Zoorb Council hear about it so fast?

There's no time to explain. End your security tour. Bring the Star Beasts back to Earth right away!

...home.

CHAPTER 2

Earth

The Pacific Ocean, close to the U.S. West Coast

The Star Beasts Drink Sanctum, Home of the Zoorb Council

The Krill are bullies. Why would the Crocs gang up with them?

As you know, in the Cosmic Creaturehood chain of command, Earth's Star Beasts outrank Pluto's Krill...

...a fact that never thrilled Pluto's leader.

CRIMES AGAINST CREATUREHOODS:

- EARTH
The Milky Way:
- Spread frostbite V13 among humans
- Provokes shrimp boat mutinies
- Stole two of Earth's satellites
- Planned attack on Dreamy World
- Attempted North Pole invasion

- POLARD
Crystalline Galaxy:
- Alleged Assassination Attempt on Polar King of Freezemark

- SERPENTINA
The C_____
- Tr_____
- A_____ multiple dens

HIGH ALERT!

HOARDS OF KRILL

KHAOS
KRILL SUPREME

DANGEROUS DICTATOR!

BRAINWASH TECHN____

Like you said, Captain, Khaos Krill is a troublemaker.

THEY MELT OUR ICE CAPS!!

NEW EXTINCT SPECIES

HUMANS

THEY DESTROY OUR HOME!!

UNLEASH THE

IN T PLA

CREATURE HIT

Khaos believes Earth's humans are the worst kind of pollution, a threat to his icy home.

When our humans downgraded Pluto to dwarf planet status, it pushed Khaos over the edge.

POLTU

PLUTO

COM LIN

M LIM

While you were stellarspeeding to Earth, Khaos' Swarm Army attacked the planet Coastica.

Khaos stole an ancient relic.

Bone...

Bye-bye.

THEY DE OUR HO

Not the Novataur fossil!

Coastica guarded a dangerous Novataur the Destroyer relic.

They weren't alone. Throughout the universe, eight Cosmic Creaturehoods protect Novataur bones.

What's Novatater the Despicable?

NOVATAUR THE DESTROYER. Did you sleep through Star Beasts Academy?

Mememe-Ahem-Ahem-MEEEEEE...

Captain, why don't I give you Zayd's SingNotes on the Novataur?

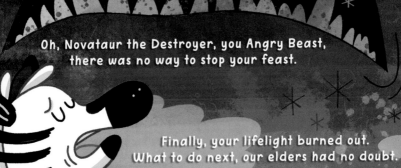

Oh, Novataur the Destroyer, you Angry Beast,
there was no way to stop your feast.

Finally, your lifelight burned out.
What to do next, our elders had no doubt.

Oh, Novataur the Destroyer,
they scattered your bones.
And to the universe, let it be known...

...re-spark the lifelight of this Angry Beast,
and your creatures will be his endless feast. ♪

Ballads get me every time.

For thousands of years, the Cosmic Creaturehood has kept the Novataur's fossils safe.

Until Khaos picked up a new hobby.

COM LINK 5

The good news is, the Krill only have one of the bones.

Make that TWO Novataur bones. The Crocodile fossil and the Coastica relic. There are six left.

Luckily, Earth's Novataur relic is protected here in this very sanctum.

Coastica needs healers. I can help. I've got Owie-Aids for days.

That's honorable of you, Karma, but we need the Star Beasts to stop the Krill.

If Khaos steals the remaining bones, he'll rebuild the Novataur and wipe out Earth's humans.

Even my human?

≶Sniff. Sniff.≶ Sounds like we need to rustle up those stray fossils.

Correct, Snuffs. From now on, all of the Novataur relics will be guarded by one planet.

The Cosmic Creaturehood Councils have agreed that Earth is the safest place to store them.

Earth's not a safe place to hide stuff! Ask any squirrel. They know what's up.

Jak2? Councilor!

Weird.

Totes weird.

Earth's Novataur fossil was on the security screen seconds ago! Where did it go?

Check the exits, Captain Bandit.

He has to be here.

Jak2?

Bye-bye.

Jak2 was rabbit-napped with the relic! The vile Krill must've gotten inside our safe room, but HOW?

The force field is password-protected, and only Zoorb Councilors know the code.

Well, flip my shell!

Hey, Unicorn. Looks like your bestie is a traitor-lope.

A traitor? Never! Jak2 is a sworn Star Beasts Councilor.

And there's no solid evidence linking him with the Krill!

Tasty Pluto treats, anyone?

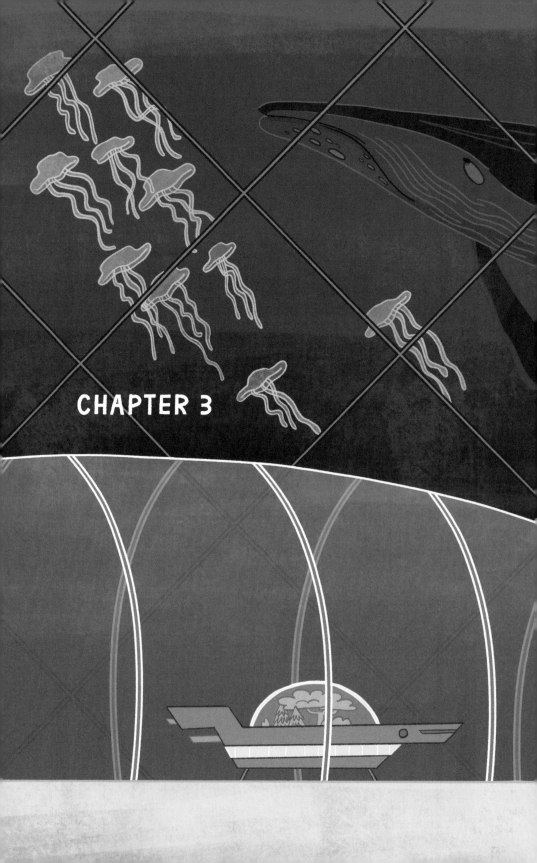

CHAPTER 3

I need to speak with Captain Bandit.

He's running an errand.

An errand? The Star Beasts are preparing to save humankind! What could be so important?

California, USA

LOST!

It's been over a year and she still misses me.

I miss her, too.

Karma:

HEADS UP, CAPTAIN.

BZZ

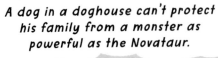

A dog in a doghouse can't protect his family from a monster as powerful as the Novataur.

I'll keep you safe, Lilly. I promise.

With so many lives at stake, the Zoorb Council decided you might need extra support.

I'm here to offer friendship and guidance.

Didn't your last friend steal Earth's Novataur bone?

Listen, Councilor, I'm more of a follow-my-nose kind of captain.

If I can't trust my sniffer, then I can't trust anything.

Captain, my greatest hope is that we can learn from each other.

Then welcome to the *Condor*, Councilor *Macca*. We could use an extra hoof on lasers.

Nebul-balls.

The Cosmic Creaturehood Planet Mesozoic

Dr. Curly, it's such an **HONOR** to meet you.

Thank you, Professor Felixraptor. It'll be *entertaining* to see the Sciencesaurs' experiments.

I can't believe it! A **TWO-TIME** Dardis winner is here on Mesozoic!

Our head scientist, Dr. Larryrex is such a fan. We've studied your... **EVERYTHING!**

Everything? Really? I should've visited sooner.

Since we're all science buds, how about we get a peek at your Novataur fossil?

Who is this *hound*?

Don't mind him. He works for me.

You asked me to lead the away crew, remember?

Yeah, but Maria, I mean, Doctor—

Then let me lead!

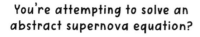

DR. MARIA CURLY? MY SCIENCE HERO!

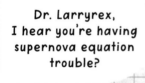

YOU'RE IN MY LAB!

Dr. Larryrex, I hear you're having supernova equation trouble?

I can't believe you said my name! I mean, YES! Can you solve it?

That's what scientists do. I'll solve your math problem if you give us your Novataur relic.

Earth? SAFE?
Don't be ridiculous, DOG.

That planet is a giant
asteroid target!

Professor, let go of the
past. This is about
survival, protecting
the future!

You pretend to be
dead for 67 million
years, then we'll talk
about survival.

We're entering the Howling Moon Galaxy!

CLICK

Shields up! Lasers ready!

Where are the Krill?

Hey, guys? I think there's something out there.

GRRRRRRRRRRRR

I can't see them on the radar.

SPOTS

Where you hiding, you big, bad growlies?

GRRRRRRRRRRRR

Wolfsbane isn't in trouble.

WE ARE!

MACCA! LASERS!

How can this be? Wolfsbane joined the Krill?

Flashtista, quick! Release the Narwhal Nebula!

Daydream gas? Not gonna work, Captain. The pilots are sealed in their ships. They won't even get a whiff.

FULL NARWHAL

1000

No noses. No problem.

Aw!
Narwhal Nebulas
are so cute!

Daydream gas as a shield?
Innovative move, Captain B.

Thanks,
but it'll only buy us
a few minutes.

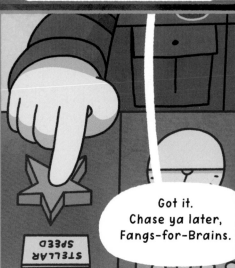

STELLAR
SPEED

Got it.
Chase ya later,
Fangs-for-Brains.

CHAPTER 4

Almost done, Captain. The *Condor* wasn't hit too crazy bad.

I've got two more circuit boards to fix. Snuffs is refilling the Narwhal Nebula tank.

There's too much smoke.

Macca, let's do another ship inspection. The *Condor* must have hidden laser damage.

≡THUMP≡

Whoops. I guess we're...

The metal bowl must've scattered my scanners! Sorry I didn't see you on my radar, little slothie.

We can't leave a baby alone on an empty planet.

The *Condor* is a fighter ship, NOT a minivan.

I have to help the last Solar Sloth of Tarda find a new home. She needs a family. I owe her that!

I can't blast baddies with a baby on board!

She's already survived a Crocodile attack.

I'm sure she can handle your flying.

Sloth hugs?

As Star Beasts Ambassador, I offer you Earth's protection and grant, um...what's your name, slothyboo?

Will "Oikos" do?

And grant Oikos a home on Earth!

But only if she's cool with that? What do you say, slothy?

Ah-ya.

Ah-ya is right!

The Krill Stronghold

Glorious Crocodiles of Lagoonta, excellent attack on Tarda. You proved your friendship yet again.

As for the Warriors of Wolfsbane, welcome to the war to end all humans!

The Wolves of the Howling Moons are honored to rage alongside the Krill.

Aaoooo! Warriors of Wolfsbane! Aaoooo!

QUIET!

Now where's that antler rabbit?

Jak2! Come forward!

Keres, find him.

With pleasure.

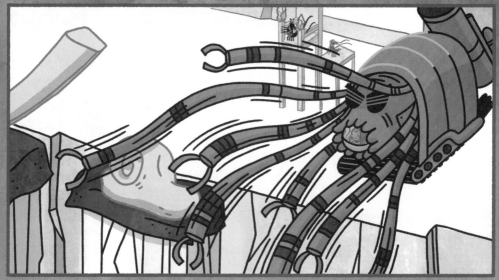

Ouch!
Hey! That
pinches!

I was on my way up there!
I had to, uh, tie my shoe!

Jackalopes
CAN hop, you know!

Jak2, my army has captured three of the Novataur's bones.

What kind of progress have you made?

Um... I finished reading a book of Novataur folk tales.

Also, Pluto's kind of chilly, so I knitted our future weapon a sweater. Don't want the Destroyer to catch a cold.

Oh! And I watched a SnoutTube video on prehistoric earwax...

You never know what might be...helpful...?

My Krill are conquering galaxies and this Earth creature is watching infomercials?

Please, Khaos. I'm attempting the impossible. It's hard to turn a myth into reality! Be patient!

Every day, humans melt Earth's polar ice caps, killing millions of our Arctic brothers and sisters.

The pollution called humans must be stopped.

If you're not smart enough to rebuild the Novataur...

...then I suggest you call a friend...

...a smarter one.

CHAPTER 5

My techie pals geek out over the Lemurs' frequency-based security system. It covers their whole planet!

SNAP

Who's a sweetie sloth? Smile for Auntie Karma!

A frequency-based security system means no phones on Conspiracy.

Destroyer Devotees don't sound interested in saving lives. There's no point negotiating with them.

To protect their relic, we've got to lean in to their culture.

Lean in to creature sacrifice? I vote to stay on the ship.

Captain Bandit and I came up with a plan! We'll sneak into the Lemur Temple...

Color me bedazzled.

...and switch out the real Novataur fossil for my replica statue!

The last thing we want to do is disturb the Lemurs.

Zayd, can you lead them in a calming meditation chant?

I'll help them tune in and zen out!

I don't feel good about the switcheroo, but at least no one will get hurt.

Captain, your plan doesn't quite follow the Star Beasts rulebook, but it has my approval.

The Cosmic Creaturehood Planet Conspiracy
The Bone Temple

My statue's a
picture-perfect copy!

Wow, Ellie!
You're so talented.

Away crew, engage.

Wait! Engage in what? I don't have a to-do!

Keep your eyes on our transport ship. We may have to leave rather quickly.

Ubi carnitas et saucepan...

Deus salt pork est browned...

Simul ergo garlic...

Et tu jalapeño, jalapeño, jalapeño...

Lime, lime, ON–IO–NS...

Anyone else craving tacos?

Ne nos mentos orange juice...

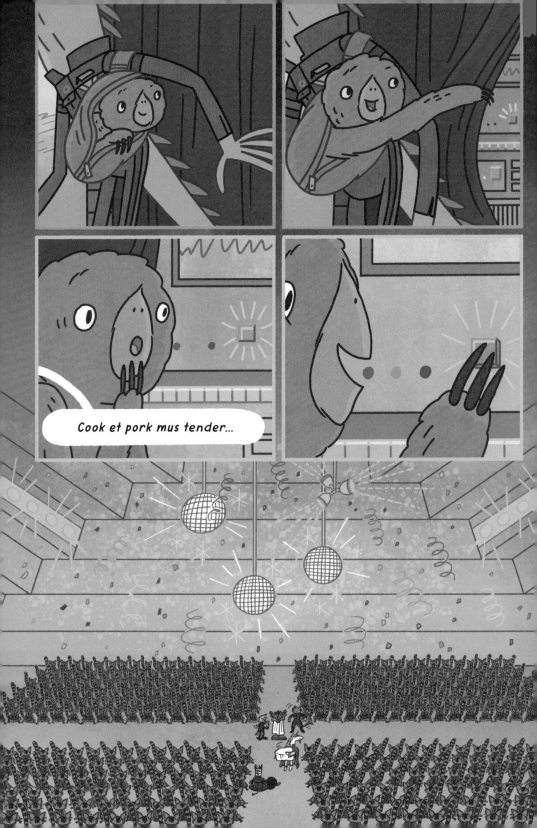

Oikos! Get back in your sloth sling!

Carnitas, carnitas, CAR-NI-T... Huh?

MOTHER STARCLUSTER!

≈HUFF≋ STAY CALM! Maybe they won't notice us?

A Ball of Doom on a meditation day! What an historic moment!

NOT in a good way.

HEY!

LASER

Snuffs! Force shields up!

Careful!

POW

Greetings, uh, Owl. I'm Star Beasts. I mean. I'm Bandit—

We received your Council's message.

The Red Shift Owls didn't need a warning about Khaos Krill. We'd already joined his cause.

My elders instructed me to deliver our Novataur the Destroyer bone to the Krill...

...to give Khaos the power he needs to end humanity.

If the Krill can destroy one species, then every creature in the universe is at risk.

I can't live with that guilt on my wings. Star Beasts, please protect us all.

I know what it's like to lose your home. Thank you...

Ofalia.

In my culture, the punishment for disobeying orders is death. I can never return to my galaxy again.

Earth welcomes you, Ofalia! Our space rock is your space rock.

Your courage reminds me of an old tune, *The Brave Beavers of Burnt End Bayou...*

Oooooooh Bayou Beavers, Burn that BBQ restaurant doooooown.

Ofalia, prepare to dock on the *Condor.*

Karma, Zayd, and Snuffs, go to the docking bay. Help Ofalia unload her cargo.

Lemurs?!?

AND we're out of Stinkeze!

Is Zayd limping?

Star Beasts to the rescue!

WAIT! Our crew will shake out the stowaways. We've got to help Ofalia get on board!

POW

Aurora-Borea-My-Alis!

Way to go, Maria!

Ofalia has docked!

Stellar it, Flashtista!

Surrender to the Swarm, Earth critters.

FIRE!

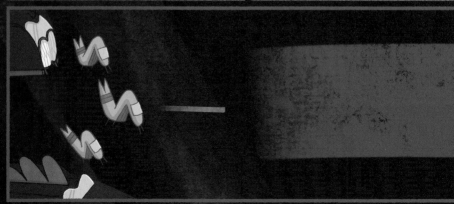

::SNIFF SNIFF::

Lemur stink.

Tell my nostrils something they don't know.

Be on guard.

The stowaways are secured, Captain.

Meet our new friends! This is Seth and Ted and Jessie and Stan and Fuzzy...

My crew rocks! We've got Ofalia and the Doc to thank, too. Come on!

Maria and I don't always see creature-to-creature, but we've got our own way of working together.

You're doggy dreamin', Bandit. That sheep only works for herself.

CHAPTER 7

Jak2 is a fool, but he was right about you.

CRASH

Khaos is going to throw me in a black hole to DIE!

WHAP

EX

EXIT

Point that thing somewhere else. I am not a shellfish!

JAB

Dr. Curly! You got my message!

I torched your message in my Bunsen burner!

I regret even reading it.

Dr. Curly, the Krill live with no regrets. Give it a try. It's quite refreshing.

You're *serious* about rebuilding the Novataur?

HA! It's a bedtime story. There's no truth to it.

Here is a truth, Dr. Curly: You care more about yourself than the Star Beasts.

We have *that* in common.

When you bring back the most powerful weapon in the universe, you'll be as famous as the Destroyer.

I'm a scientist, not an executioner!

Dr. Curly, I only care that you're a professional and that you GET THE JOB DONE.

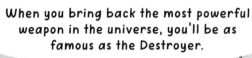

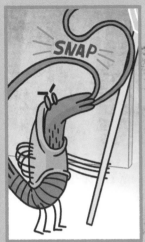

SNAP

CRASH!!

You have one hour to re-spark Novataur the Destroyer and bring it back to life.

FLEX

Don't make me have to motivate you.

SLAM!

I stand with science, not with creeps!

131

The Novataur isn't science, Dr. Curly. It's magic! I'll show you!

Do you know any old bone spells?

SCREECH

Spells? Are you blue-lipped batfish crazy?

I read a fable that said bone spells could summon more sparks like these.

BUMP

They might be interstellar fairy dust!

Bless my beakers. I've seen this before!

If I can improve the Sciencesaurs' experiment...

DRAG

...then I can stop Khaos!

BUMP

ONE HOUR LATER...

This new Frankensteined bone should do the trick.

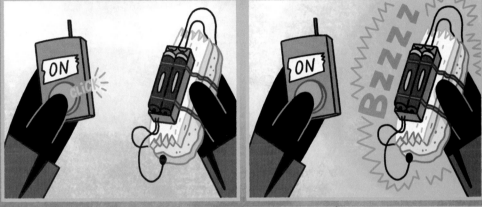

YES!

I've invented DAZZLE MATTER!

Dazzle matter? Don't you mean dark matter?

133

It's ALIVE!

I love science.

Earth will be MINE!

SWING

What's wrong with my prize?

Is he allergic to Pluto pollen, or is this his new normal?

There's nothing normal about a space zombie.

The Novataur is a billion years old. He's going to have some tics.

Aches, pains, fossil spams, you never know what might flare up.

Star Beasts! Extra security has been added to the Safe Room. Bring the Novataur's relics at once!

Dr. Curly has betrayed the Star Beasts.

Maria would never sell us out!

Face it. The Doc's gone Krill. She cares more about her chemistry set than our crew.

Does Khaos have all the Destroyer relics?

For certain. He's probably rebuilding the Novataur as we speak.

To save our humans, we have to attack the Krill Stronghold!

Excuse me, Councilor Feng, here. Attacking a castle might not be the answer. Snuffs? Are you there?

zzzzzz≥SNORT!≨zzzPOTATOES...

Yes! Jumpin' Jupiter Jelly! I'm here!

Do you have any cruciferous vegetables in your space garden?

Yeah. There's some broccoli leftover from Stir-Fry Friday.

Perfect! Go to Dr. Curly's lab. Grab a test tube labeled CASA 102. Don't spill a drop!

What's your plan, Councilor Feng?

Novataur the Destroyer!

The Destroyer's energy field is messing with our radar! Earth's satellites won't pick it up, either!

Snuffs, grab the broccoli.

Let's supernova sauté that Destroyer!

CHAPTER 8

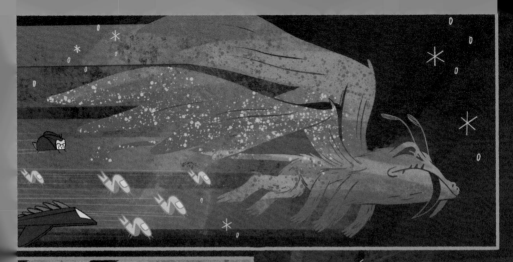

The Novataur's bones are like atomic armor, but I built in a way around that skeleton!

In fact, inventing dazzle matter is probably my greatest scientific achievement to date.

When it kicks in, my dazzle matter will rattle the Destroyer's bones, making them come loose!

You'll see the creature's dark matter core. Blasting the core is the only way to stop the Novataur!

How will we know when the dazzle matter kicks in?

I can't confirm this, but it will probably look like a burst of light.

Confirmed.

Any minute now, the Novataur's dark matter could absorb my dazzle matter. The clock is ticking.

I'm sorry for stealing the relic! Don't let me die! I'll be a better bunny. I promise.

Thanks for your help, Doctor.

That's what Star Beasts do, Captain.

No hand cramps.
No hand cramps.

You got this, Pep!
Khaos is so focused
on the Novataur,
he won't even
notice us.

Right.
I've got this.

Everyone keep your tails
crossed, just in case.

Smooth flying, Pep-peroni!

Here comes the dazzle matter!

Almost there.

Steady, Pep!

SWAT!!!

Oh—

DINK

BAM!

Star Beasts!

WAR SWARM!
WAR SWARM!

CHAPTER 9

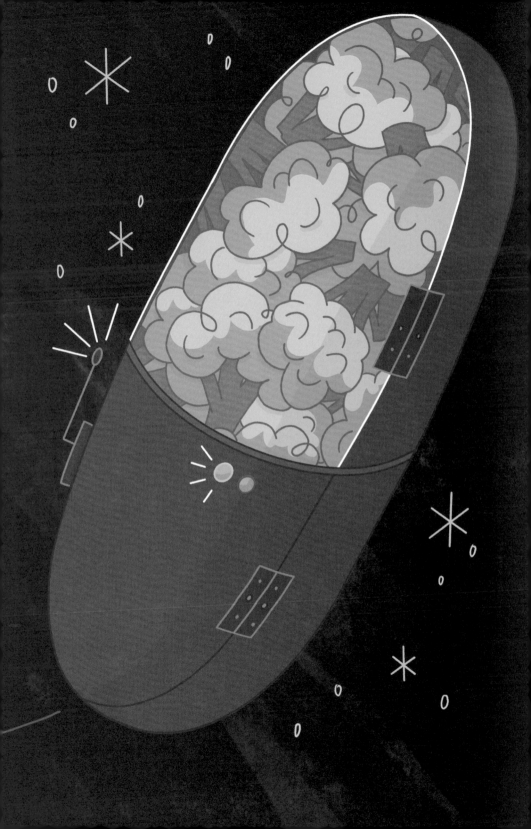

Karma!

Force shields are up, Bandit!

BOOM

Mythic blasting, Macca-corn!

Alas! It wasn't me!

Greetings, crew! We'll fight the Swarm. You focus on the Destroyer!

Captain, Pod Two is ready to launch, but there's a traffic jam in the way.

Flashtista, fly around that hot mess. Get us close to the Novataur.

Is that wise? You saw what happened to that Krill ship. The Destroyer flung it into deep space.

Don't worry. I've got a Plan B.

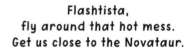

"B" stands for "Better work," right?

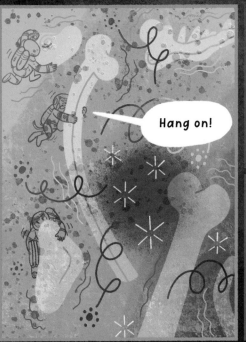

Hang on!

ZAP!

Go ahead.
Blast us again.

I triple-turtle
dare you.

The dark matter core!

I CAN DO THIS.

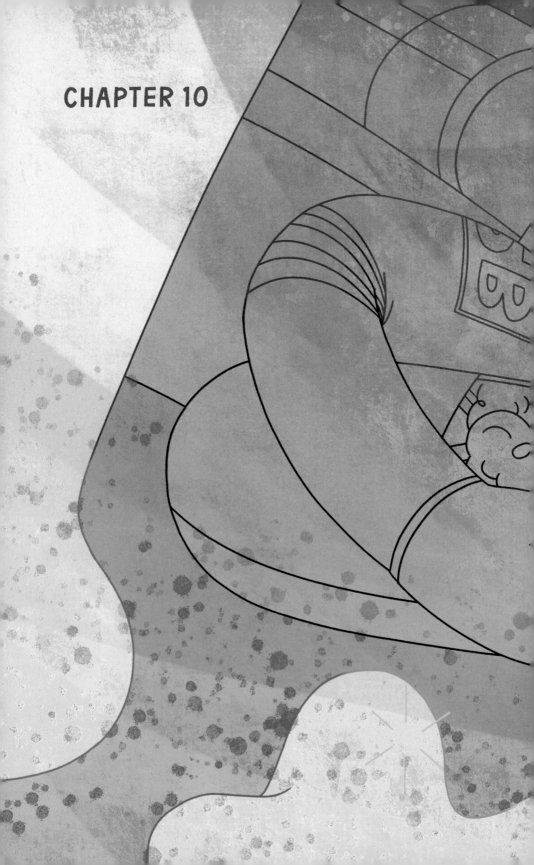

CHAPTER 10

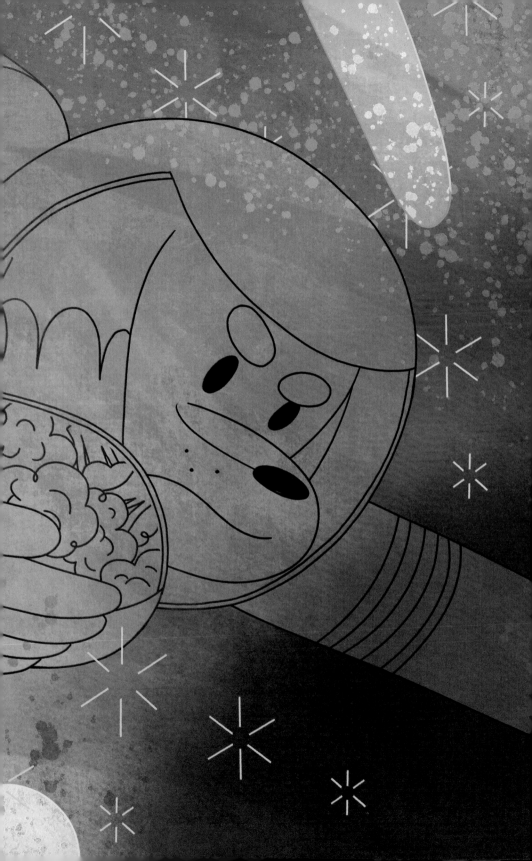

The Star Beasts saved the universe.

BEEP
BEEP

Nice work, Captain.

No hand cramps.
No hand cramps.

Are you sure no one can see the *Condor*?

Hello?

Helloooo?

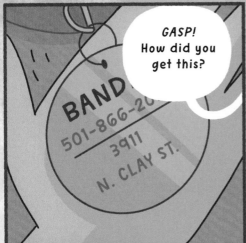

THANKS TO...

Star Beasts wouldn't be *Star Beasts* without the support, encouragement, and know-how of **JOHN D. YOUNG**. You are the stardust beneath the *Condor*'s stellarspeed.

KYLE STRAHAM
for being our guide to the comic industry cosmos.

AMY BEBERMEYER
for her supernova spell-check skills.

LISA HADLEY
for being a far-out color flatter.

THE FARRIS FAMILY:
galactic business manager, **ART**, hostess with the mostest, **BECKY**, and social media master, **LYNLEY**.

AMANDA MEADOWS
for believing in our pulsar potential
and having such cool glasses.

Our kick-asteroid agent, **FIONA KENSHOLE**.

VINTAGE PHOENIX, THE COMIC CAVE, ELITE,
and all the comet-blazin' comic shops that stocked early issues.

The best librarian in the universe, **JESSIE EAST**.

And most importantly, thank you to all our friends, family, and fans who cheered on *Star Beasts* from launch to liftoff

ALLYSON LASSITER

is an illustrator, plush designer, bike rider, and soup-maker. She likes meteor showers, soft-serve ice cream, dogs, and triple-quasar-style dance moves.

STEPHANIE YOUNG

is a writer, pancake connoisseur, and pie baker. She likes the constellation Pleiades, mint chip ice cream, cats, and funny space lingo (WHAT THE HUBBLE?).

All creatures must follow their destiny. Let's discover yours!

Using your birth month, the day you were born, and the first letter of your last name, decode your personal Star Beasts mission!

YOUR BIRTH MONTH

JANUARY: Seek

FEBRUARY: Save

MARCH: Conquer

APRIL: Battle

MAY: Protect

JUNE: Heal

JULY: Explore

AUGUST: Celebrate

SEPTEMBER: Study

OCTOBER: Investigate

NOVEMBER: Fight

DECEMBER: Honor

DAY YOU WERE BORN

01: Space
02: Crescent
03: Galactic
04: Dark Matter
05: Dwarf
06: Lunar
07: Meteoroid
08: Shooting Star
09: Sun
10: Cosmic
11: Nebula
12: Eclipse
13: Star
14: Milky Way
15: Asteroid
16: Celestial
17: Outer Rim
18: Global
19: Orbiting
20: Moon
21: Big Bang
22: Deep Space
23: Meteor
24: Solar
25: Universal
26: Dazzle Matter
27: Telescopic
28: Crater
29: Sky
30: Pulsar
31: Black Hole

FIRST LETTER OF YOUR LAST NAME

A: Kittens
B: Tacos
C: Ladybugs
D: Elephants
E: Donuts
F: Lizards
G: Parrots
H: Puppies
I: Caterpillars
J: Giraffes
K: Snakes
L: Sloths
M: Hurricanes
N: Ferrets
O: Penguins
P: Blizzards
Q: Whales
R: Lions
S: Narwhals
T: Rainbows
U: Pizza
V: Horses
W: Popsicles
X: Hamsters
Y: Bears
Z: Nachos

Let's see... my destiny is... SEEK DWARF LIZARDS! I love seeking!!

Before *Star Beasts* was a novel, it was a sneak peek comic!
Early fans will remember this little adventure.

Whiskers and Kirby are Steph and Lassie's real-life pets and helped inspire *Star Beasts*.

Fun Fact: The Biodome on the *Condor* makes it possible for Snuffs to farm, even in space.

Steph and Lassie truly believe ice cream is an investment in happiness.
Their recommendations? Coconut vanilla and mint chip.

Please notice how Karma is using the Narwhal Nebula correctly on this page.

If Bandit hadn't joined the Star Beasts crew, here are some other dogs who were almost captain.